RECIPES FROM THE RED PLANET

RECIPES FROM THE RED PLANET

Meredith Quartermain

Graphics by Susan Bee

BookThug
2010

Department of Narrative Studies No. 4

FIRST EDITION
copyright © Meredith Quartermain, 2010
graphics © Susan Bee, 2010

The production of this book was made possible through the generous assistance of The Canada Council for The Arts and The Ontario Arts Council.

Canada Council for the Arts   Conseil des Arts du Canada   ONTARIO ARTS COUNCIL   CONSEIL DES ARTS DE L'ONTARIO

Cover: Susan Bee, *The Red Door*, oil and collage on linen, 2008. Collection: Paul Auster and Siri Hustvedt.

LIBRARY AND ARCHIVES CANADA CATALOGUING IN PUBLICATION

Quartermain, Meredith, 1950-
        Recipes from the red planet / Quartermain,
Meredith ; Susan Bee, illustrator.

(Department of narrative studies ; no. 4)
ISBN 978 1 897388 65 5

        I. Bee, Susan II. Title. III. Series: Department of narrative studies ; no. 4.

PS8583.U335R43 2011   C813'.6   C2010-904503-3

For Robin

It's as if a Martian comes into a room with children's blocks with A, B, C, D, E which are in English and he tries to convey a message. This is the way the source of energy goes. But the blocks, on the other hand, are always resisting it.

– *Jack Spicer*

TABLE OF CONTENTS

HOTEL NARRATIVE

She said and he thought and he did and she thought and he said and she did and they thought and I went and they said and you heard and we saw and they wanted and she didn't think and you didn't see and I felt and he liked and we said we couldn't tell. Said Mr. Narrator to Mrs. Narrator. Said trialogue. And Mrs. Narrator thought Mr. Narrator thought Lady Agonist thought Mr. Narrator. Said Lord Agonist to the psychiatrist thought Mr. Narrator. Lacked character said Lady Agonist said Mrs. Narrator thought Lord Agonist. Are you for or against Agonist said Mrs. Narrator to the dog thought Mr. Narrator against Lady Agonist's thigh. I wanted Mr. Narrator to think Lady Agonist felt Mrs. Narrator had Mr. Narrator by the. Her Ladyship felt Lord Agonist didn't. Behind the ears then under a nipple inserted in her pocket. Thought Mrs. Narrator. Would your Lordship care for some. Bushes near a lake, mound at a mineshaft, peak with an outing. Bottoms up her Ladyship's butter, we said. And breadfruit. Is your Lordship out. They think he's in. Mr. Narrator. Thought I. Said Mrs. Narrator. His Lordship's out of pocket. Her Ladyship's innuendo. He's out to lunch. She's ins and outs. He's *in futuro* incognito. Out of debt. Incomplete. Mrs. Narrator dreamt her Ladyship's buttons wanted setting forth to switchboard for room service his Lordship. Keeps falling asleep. Said Mr. Narrator. Thought Mrs. Narrator. Don't tell me I'm fresh towel check-out his Lordship. Said her Ladyship's buttony TV. Thought. Mrs. Narrator. You're going to soap the doorman I wanted to this morning. Do you have a reservation we could telephone. Mr. Narrator's bellhop. Not that that would. The black that that she mailed that you said we'd already said. Said Mrs. Narrator thought his Lordship. Not that. The other that that I said Lady Agonist said she'd like to have felt. Not *that*.

THE PLACKENER

Mother's Day and Workers' Day, battlegrounds, lost cities, massacres. Trophies for motorboats, baseball players, horses. Persephone hijacked to the underworld, gothic reed-houses of Uruk. These are my stuff, these layers pasted on, stuck together, pieced in reindeer horn, china relief, gold enameling. Jade sealing orifices of a corpse. Medallions for martingales. Open-work tortoise-shell, Sèvres porcelain, Medici porcelain, hinged platelets. Words commemorating lost spaces and quixotic battles of tongue and sense I plackener match hunchfully to my lake of tangents. Row here row there – pause, oars dripping, to contemplate the city jigsawed on the sky – its columns of noble knobs and notches interlocking plaques, flittered by millions of silently moving lips. One by one, I gather sky-pieces, stand them up – a set of tin soldiers, a toy zoo of dinosaurs, a troupe of She Things, Tank Women, Elastigirls, Moondragons. Oh my moral fibers, my spirits and dispositions, my quixotic combatants, soar across my universe and bring me news of eccentricity.

RAIN

You'll take me as I come. I slick the streets, shush the wheels. Splat the plaid and black umbrellas. I hammer. I belt. Dribble and drip. On hair, on slicks, on sodden shoes. I laden twigs with dropkins, darken walls, glisten roofs, douse the feathers of chimney-hunching crows. Not the house that Jack built, not the mason that laid the brick, nor the architect that hired the mason, nor the god that hired the architect. I swamp a vacant lot, its concrete steps to nonexistent bungalow. Beat its absent window-panes, its haggard shrubs with batter, pound, and thump. Knock its dearthy lack of shingles, its truant walls. Hulloo, anybody there? Here's weather-words for nobody-ness. Master Void and Madam Vacuum. Lord and Lady Emptiful. How do you do? Enchanté. What a splendid tabula rasa, what grand views of Non-attendance Peak! I don't mind a glass of No-man's-land champagne. And yes, I'll have a plate of null-set cakes in hearthless nothinghood. I'm not unhappy you're unamused with this nonentity naughtdom. Please may I inconsider myself negatelessly at your antidisposal, your sublimely abyssful blankship.

MY NATURE

In it I looked igneous and sedimentary. Elk rutted there and bears ambled. The latest maples were the most sought after. Would you like solid, liquid or gas trousers, my servant asked, An animal, vegetable or mineral chemise? I donned moody sentences, full of boisterous reserve yet I hankered for clouds that were neither stratus nor cirrus, nor nimbus nor cumulus.

I will leave my nature, I said to my servant, I will leave my trendy reptiles and spiders, my mock oranges and false foxgloves. I don't want to be natural. I will step out the gates of my nature.

I have packed your valise, said my servant, Here is a lunch of fairy shrimps and coconut crabs. Keep this flask of suchness with you at all times. Do not leave it beside any Georgian Bays, Edwardian Bays or Victorian ones. Do not leave it near Milk Rivers, Powder Rivers, Rock Rivers or Back Rivers. Do not leave it in any Laurentian Mountains or Pyramid Lakes.

Goodbye, my nature, I sang, as I headed out the gate. Farewell, my customary rawness, my authentic naivety, my endangered sparrows and warblers, my cotton-, silk- and ribbonwood trees. And the road faded away in every direction.

If I were you, said a voice, I wouldn't be so moody.

If you were me, who would I be then?

If I were you, I would have traded me that lunch for some pointlessness.

Immaterial, I said as my spontaneous instinctive native repast rambled off with the flask of suchness and I whirled fortuitously, redundantly, adscititiously – longing for Extraneous Islands, for Incidental City, for the Dominion of Alienage – back through my virgin warp.

BANKING

Of course I wore my prison uniform as I walked through the streets to the bank. I felt right at home with the African zebras stenciled on the stripes of the zebra walk. Black and white; man and woman, shouted the crosswalk. I was not black or white; I was a zebra in a land where everyone was striped. At the bank, I joined the line-up of other prisoners watching television screens above the tellers – a hand in a food-show swirling thick white icing onto cupcakes, beside flames and smoke and faces in a Baghdad street. We prisoners stood in rows inside the velvet ropes to the tills. A skateboarder told us about himself: The best is at night, up on Main-Street hill, I head down to the ocean, I go and go 20 maybe 30 blocks no cars, I zigzag, go loop the loop, crisscross all those white lines. When women go past my construction site, said a man in a hardhat and cement-splattered boots, I never whistle, I always lift my hat – humans should act civilized; that's why we have skyscrapers. It's amazing (a hairdresser spoke up) how all the condos are the same little cells; yet each one is decorated differently, like human heads. Just then a blizzard of coconut chips whirled down on the gooey heads of a dozen cupcakes, and a phalanx of police in helmets, masks and shields marched down a burning street over the tellers at their wickets. An angora sweater and bangles tallying her receipts; a jacket and tie explaining there's nothing the bank can do about your pension that wasn't deposited this month; and a troll, though not as large as the ones in *Peer Gynt,* explaining loan options at very reasonable rates near the bars to the safety deposit boxes, which remained loudly shut.

ROAD TRIP

I back the car, drive down the highway in reverse. Warehouses, fields, cows, electricity pylons rush away. I roll along – five reverse gears. The highest backs at 90 mph – steering with side mirrors big as TVs. No fear of rear-enders. If anyone tries to, I can see them through my windscreen and honk. Or for fun I can make a double rear-ender with the car ahead, tail-pipe to tail-pipe, like two insects sharing abdominal fluids. I drive along, watch my TVs – surprised looks on drivers' faces. I shrug, raise my eyebrows, briefly lift my hands from the wheel. Hey, I say, It's no different than rowing a boat. You face away from where you're going. Front is back. Back is front. Ahead is behind. No left turn is no right turn. Vancouver becomes Slavic Vancouver. MOXY 108 is 801 YXOM. HA HA = AH AH. You're going to OOM not MOO. You watch the deeps limit, don't want to exceed 18. Looking for the WAXY exit, you find YXAW is not far from YTTAT and TOXIT. And Canada's become a country that rhymes with a mountain range in New York State.

CANADA

This is why we drive, why we celebrate, why the worst bullying happens in groups, and why we stand on borders, we yawn, say eh, why we do statistics and grow horses. This is why we need government, we do assessments and workouts, Royal Commissions, we bother, eat donuts, why we brag about winter, do broadcasts, play hockey. This is why we eat cod-liver oil and back-bacon, why we sweep ice, call it cultural capital. Why route rhymes with boot and not clout. Why we grow 8 million hectares of wheat and play baseball, we make domestic products, die of cancer and heart attacks instead of bombs or famine. Why our sea-to-sea store sells tires, we don't spell perimeter like metre or honour like motor. This is why we sell oil and gas, not coffee or computers, why we have armed services and forestry, armorial bearings, the fur trade, parties and ice-breakers. Why we have maple syrup, lions holding maple leaves, we have occupations and food-rules, we go into space with unicorns waving fleurs-de-lis. It's why we work like beavers, not eagles, chew and dam on average 10 hours a week for personal care, which is why we tattoo ourselves, deke out of kerfuffles, get pissed about ridings. Why we put rubbers on our feet. It's why anglophones telephone francophones. This is why we drive clicks, not mphs, wearing tuques on our zeds and toonies on our cheques. It's why we have freight-rates and margarine wars, why police ride steeds, we eat 175 kilos of veg a year and potatoes are veg, trans is a highway or a fat. We can send a letter one click or 6000 for half a loonie which is or isn't crazy for selves at odds with our brains.

L'AMANTE ANGLAISE

She flirted with her. She put her tongue to her liquorice. She tasted a négligé, a chemise, some culottes, a pelisse. Plunged into ravines, scaled buttes, traversed escarpments and plateaus. Of la belle française.

Les complications arose. La française ne l'a pas aimé! Votre prononciation est terrible! Take your tongue from my words. My mots in your closette minuscule put back. And don't forget: give back my camisole and peignoir.

Oh, how would she escape her armoire anglaise into the outness of la française?! Furieuse, elle a crié, They're not yours; they're mine. You can't have them.

Imbécile! Don't you know French when elle vous donne un coup sur la tête? Besides you look stupide in that lace. Comme une mêlée chartreuse. A fricassée de polkadots.

Then give me back le weekend and le hotdog. Le film, le punk and le squat.

Mais la belle française ensconced herself in une silk sulk.

Pourquoi won't you couchez avec moi, you know perfectly well our great great grandmother gave me that chemise in 1066. Pourquoi must you be une puriste? Couchez avec moi dans le downtown. Couchez avec moi dans le camping. Couchez avec moi on my couch.

BECOMING A WAITRESS

This is the restaurant where I'm learning to be a waitress. I study the tables and chairs. So very antique. The Martians shift them easily, or sometimes not for days. I like it when Martians leave omens on the plates. This blini reminds me of the Queen, Mr. Sun-face will say to his partner, the Stick Insect, who's staring at a vinaigrette like a spy in a heroin lab. Her majesty's wearing a crown and earrings – the eye-holes are a little small, I'll add some caviar mascara. A Plaid Tie will fork his pasta seaweed and fish the ragoût for his Cuban aunt. At finishing camp, Madame Vegan will say, we never served striped risotto with turnip emulsion.

The chef tunes her radio to Martian reality. Boiling with rage and parsley while the maître d' poaches rabbits and the hostess cooks books. This is when I listen for recipes from the red planet – little incogency custards and latent tajines to arrange my cutlery and wine glasses: All that glitters keeps the doctor away from eating your cake. A penny saved speaks louder than too many broths. When the cat's away count your chickens before you leap. Better late than eggs in spilt milk.

24

There's the owner – Mr. Spicer – in the Armani suit and gold rings. He's teaching me to take orders. Prostrate before an altar. I will kneel, I will kiss hands, I will become ordinary. When you take the orders, he says, be playful with your bishops – which one is the most tastefully laced. Which one wants a shield with his swordfish. A Petit Manseng with his pork tenderloin, his raw oysters, his chili con carne.

CLOUDS

I thought about clouds and earth. Electricities hold each other prisoner. I thought fondly and fallen. That touching the earth is fog. Entángled business – no, not business – yes, busyness. Last summer uncloudedly happy for an Italian frieze. I thought about night visitors to cloudberries. Puffs of ice cream and tower blocks. I thought in disgrace, in secrecy, unknowingly. My flock straying west or east grazed episodically the movement of history's saturated conditions all grey and cozy and introverts insided. Molecules of mind jam a cloud with coherence. You can't hold a cloud in your pocket, stuff it in a plastic bag or suitcase but between thumb and middle finger, I thought, opens a lake and Cloud Island directly in its mouth. I thought of OE *clud* a rocky hill ripening on the female cloudberry. I wandered lonely as, and under a. Billowing. Rapidly deepening surface. The higher the turbidity the more scattering and densely boisterous. I thought, my flock shall not want for smudged horizons hung over forageable prospects. You can pick cloudberries when they're still hard, I thought, and store them under water. Millions of thoughts deluge the clouder. Thoughts opposite charges top and bottom browse the field's static textures. Clear weather to the stables where horses come to work, eat a cloud or two and carrots float in blue and birds and cats.

IN SEARCH OF A PLAQUE,

I walk a cemetery of soggy grass, wet low sky, old cedars drooping their rain-sodden arms, for king raven bending a top tip. I walk avenues of stones, yellow leaves, red rain-dropped bushes. Hills of graves roll up to the sky. To ocean inlet. Blue mountains massively loom. Over Block 0, Plot 5, Lot 1. Her grave a patch of grass, next to a hedge and the small obelisk of the Evans family. A woman pushes her baby carriage past mounds of dirt and plywood sheets over holes.

What would she have said, my Nightingale, had she left a memo on a stony, scrolly lectern, or a line on a granite pillow. *Just asleep. A short nap. With friends. Stepped out for some milk. In God's garden. Carrots need weeding.* A postcard from her trip, *Crossing good. Jotted this on the ferry. My journey just begun. Expedition Under.* A telegram for weather's edits – *end must art __sting ____fully __ever _____ lost in ___odyl's _____den* – under a proscenium arch of floral curtains, an angel flying on a pedestal. Fanny Dalrymple Redmond, Nurse and Deaconess, Founder, Vancouver's first hospital for women and children. Amid gothic canopies and granite monuments, rococo Italian busts, headstones bedsteads. Teach us, "immortal Bird."

A MARIJUANA STALK

Unbeknownst to the woodsman, a marijuana stalk has grown 20 feet over the summer. The first snow has wilted its leaves. The woodsman cuts it down and hangs it to dry in his cabin, pocketing his pipe and some hashish. A smoke for later, he thinks, on a path through a meadow, down a road to a frosty dock – floating out to a raft of sail boats in a lake. He walks down the icy planks, then turns to the grey water sliding murkily around clumps of snowy reeds. In a swift, decisive movement, he jumps in, becomes completely submerged, then rises to the surface, pulls himself up on the dock and sits there, drenched clothes streaming around him. Come, get out of the cold, do come inside, the narrator calls to him, the narrator afraid to set foot on the frosty planks of the floating dock. Why, he shouts back. I suppose, the narrator says, You've heard of pneumonia. The woodsman jumps off the dock and dives under the grey brown water toward a steep bank of tangled snowy bushes, leaving the narrator wondering how she will speak to her character. Is a narrator to her woodsman like a king to his army, or a mother to a son. Devil to disciple, or god to bewitched. Like language to word, or planet to plant?

MY KITCHEN

In my copper-bottom pans, I stir up little reductions. My blender chops, grinds, whips and liquefies. Here you can push my buttons. Make some cookies on my sheets.

I love my cupboards full of bowls and plates. I get half-crocked, then completely crocked, serve myself in china, pottery, crystal, or teak, following the newspaper style section. Or, loathing the style section, lay myself in tableware of plaid and polka-dot. A piece of grandmother Higginsbottom, a patch of uncle Fopsky, a scrap of great-aunt Winderland, clashing salt and pepper sets, sprinkling myself far too liberally in stews and pastries.

What platters and gravy boats have I not washed in this sink of myself! What pickle dishes, tureens and side plates! Dunking them in the sudsy circuitry of my motherboard.

Would you like to touch my stove – everything's on the back burner. My oven's almost new. I had a bun in it once. I called a repairman. He said he'd fix it if I wore my hair ever after like Betty Crocker. I let him in, let him turn my dials under the oven light. I'm quite excited he said, jumping up and down. He got his foot tangled in my racks.

A DINNER PARTY

Here's a Roman host, bon vivant, forgetting to introduce the poet who's the wife of the MP to the psychologist who's the husband of the editor, in scarves and coats, at the front door, with bags of wine that may or may not have been expensive. The Etruscan hostess leans toward the modish art historian and the professor of 20th-century literature. The Greek poet shifts her drapery and demurs to the Persian psychologist. Coats and gloves are off, hung in closets, over newel post, on chairs or even floors. "I take exception to this museum, I find it balky and protestable, whoever runs it, let's be against them" – the poet carries a vase on her head or Athena's crested helmet – "I'd rather not be wearing these snakes; they're tickling my breasts." "Oh what a fine snakelace" – the MP reaches to grasp it in his fingers: "it was my wedding gift to her," he announces. "Here's to the museum" – the professor, adroitly adjusts his panther-skin and his crown of vines, then raises a bunching cascade of grapes. "Cups cups cups, for everyone – where would I be without my pine-cone!" "And where would I be without my face that launches a thousand puppy dogs," Art History demands, passing the bucket of ice to Psyche's Logistics Man who's just now extending his wings and flexing his bow. The arrow flies – "I'm only performing myself today; I have no sympathy for anyone who chooses to live in a museum." "You must do something to your palate," beams the rosy-cheeked host into the tangled intimations and gestures of his guests. Plates fly over knives and forks with servings too large, too small, too meaty, too veggie, too red, too blue. What story are they broiling in? More salad? More sex? More slices? More sycophants? Oh, yes please, they're delicious, what a good cook you are, may I have the recipe? The hostess gazes fondly at her dessert dishes, each one an infant Hermes about to steal a lot of cattle. "I'm so glad I brought my diadem and scepter" – the Overseer of Publishing slips a pomegranate to the Forth-Holding Chatterer. "And I my Trojan Horse" intones the Mistress of Things Deemed Fine. At last they all find coats and hats. The hostess waves goodbye in her multi-braided head – "And do, oh do bring your imaginary guests next time too."

THE LAW LIBRARIAN

is new to the firm, taking over from Miss Spinks who died, and it is she who must stop the law books from disappearing forever in the lounges, board rooms, associate's offices, photocopy rooms, and lairs of the partners. Once a month you will please audit the library and retrieve all missing books, the managing partner and the chief accountant instruct her, in their dark blue suits and crisp silk ties (she wears straight black skirt, white blouse, sensible pumps). Nighttime while the partners wine and dine, she sets off with her wire trolley. In ancient Greece, she'd have cleaned stables of 3000 cattle or collected golden fleece from a herd of sun-crazed, furious sheep. Stockwell, Q.C. She unlocks the door. Here she might've fought three-headed dogs or a stygian sleep. But no, there they are – the missing *Criminal Law* by Fraudster and *Equity Law* by H.R.H. Oil. And here's another – how surprising to find it among Stockwell's hunting trophies and gun racks: *A History of the Common Law* by Joan Miró. She fingers its amazing maps of figures and lines. Begins writing a note to Stockwell: *Bravo! Bravo for choosing such a book.* A jingle sounds in the passage. She steps out on the patio, then climbs the rose trellis to the patio above. A man on his cell-phone: *No I don't want the property without the tenants, you keep bringing this up and I keep telling you.* The librarian slides open his patio door, his vast apartments open to other grander arrangements of couches, vases, fireplaces, gold, glass, silver, bronze, oak. At last she finds the entrance, with its double teak doors, which for her is an exit.

HE IMAGINED A SEAWALL

James Cunningham, stonemason, born on the Isle of Bute in the Firth of Clyde, with its Buttock Point and Garroch Head, its lochs and burns and glens and Druids, its Norsemen and Scots, its grey granite at Kilchattan susceptible of high polish, its Dunoon phyllites, its grits, schists, sills and bosses, its Suidhe Hill of olivine-basalt. He was 32 when he boarded ship in Glasgow and sailed or steamed down Firth of Clyde past his former island, now entirely possessed by the Marquess of Bute, whose ancestor, Prime Minister under George III, was so reviled for his taxes he could only move about with a band of prize-fighters. James Cunningham crossed the Atlantic to the New Scotland. Here there were no marquesses. He had with him a good set of mallets, saws and chisels, the world being a matter of footings and slip joints, of dressing, coping and moulding. He disembarked in Halifax, the Mi'kmaq called it Chebucto. He strolled past piers and docks, a sugar refinery, an oil refinery, a market and department store, up to the citadel, its wrought-iron gates, its rubble wall capped with slabs of granite. The long and short work in the ashlar faces of shipping firms, banks, churches – so Glaswegian, he felt right at home, though he didn't like hammer-dressed quoins on brick.

But look at the voussoirs and joggled joints in that architrave! The cornices and parapets along the roofs! Oddly there was no work in Halifax for stonemasons. Go west, his landlady said. Go west honey, said the naughty ladies on Water Street. Go west, said the red-coated navy men, the moving pictures, the cod on the flakes. Take the train to Calgary, get farm land. In sunny Alberta. *I'm not a farmer,* he said to his landlady, *I'm a stonemason.* Well then, and I'm a concert pianist, she brushed up toast crumbs from the table-cloth. *Does it go all the way to British Columbia,* he asked the conductor, *I don't want Alberta.* He got off at the salt-smell, the damp mellow air and smudged light of a coast. Banks, hotels, armories, export/import firms to build. *I can unwrap my spirit level,* he thought, *my bevels and plumb bobs.* He opened their canvas swaddlings, laid out squares, rules and trowels. Just then England got into a great war, he boarded the train heading east, steamed back across the Atlantic to build transepts and apses in the rubble of trenches, a plinth and lintel of sandbags, a dovetailed mortise on a plank bridge. He was not killed. He returned to the waves bashing some British rocks or sometimes just gently caressing a place where they spoke Sḵwx̱wú7mesh. Unwrapped his thoughts and dreams, a scabbling hammer and chisels. *I'll make a dam to hold back the trees and keep out the sea.* Hundred-pound blocks from outcrops below tide-line. Granite full of sap like cut apple he sawed and split and shaped, wedging rubble stones with snecks. Gently and lavishly mortaring. Chips and spalls fell away. He was 40, 45, 55, 65. He was let go from the community of paid artisans, having built a library and a chemistry lab. Still he went on with his land buttress. The sea came in, licked the stones, liked what it tasted. The sea went out, baring barnacles and mussels and kelp. He squeezed along the rocky shore running his hands over mortar and chiseling. Passed an old sea-stack Skwxwú7mesh said was once a man. *Stone-man, I will finish my wall.* No you won't, said stone-man, you're 85, you'll stop dead in your footprints like me. James Cunningham, says the plaque near the old stack. Folks called him Jimmy.

A DISAGREEMENT OVER LUNCH

She passes him more cheese and slices of ham, suggesting that ants
are quite amazing architects. He believes, on the contrary, that
Architecture has a history. An eggplant or it might be a football
enters the dining room and floats blimplike over the lunch table.
But surely, she says, ants in their cities practice architecture just as
we do. The eggplant puffs itself and hatches some red balloons. No
no no, he says, Architecture chooses design, materials, location,
Architecture is deliberative. Flags and streamers sprout from the
eggplant. It zooms around the diners, grazing their spectacles.
But do humans *choose* to build skyscrapers, she wonders, over
the crabcakes, or do they *have* to build them, the same way all
over the planet. The eggplant hovers over a bowl of peaches, it
lets down ladders and rope, disembarking tiny passengers. He
pours another glass of wine, allowing that humans looked at
from Mars have their uniformities, but looked at from Earth, we
see creation, invention, originators. But surely ants have their
Palladios and Vitruviuses, she rejoins. The eggplant lifts out of the
fruit bowl and floats dejectedly above it. Convoys and caravans
of passengers trudge over peachy hills.

40

If ants do it, then what on earth would *architecture* mean?

There's an eggplant or a football in the fruit bowl.

It looks like a blimp.

It's moving around.

It's hatching eggs.

Wagon trains crawling the peaches.

Ants.

No, they're tiny humans.

ISLANDS

Today I'm going to an island and for that I'm completely green, a light bottle green, lime in some lights, malachite or verdigris in others. I'm sea and pea and new-lumber heading out to my island isn't land. An olive applish village green. For my jadely budding antlers. What a taut present tense, high strung, walking its rope with balancing rod! Little boats ferry me to my isn't country and stubborn-factdom. Little boats, the Spirit of George McInnes, the Spirit of Nora O'Grady plying a False Creek – names for impossible truths, for ghosts leaking Irish Wicklow Knockananna, Knockanarrigan, the squiggled Avonbeg river, and hulking hills of Mullaghcleevaun. Ah Nora, Nora, *Dia 's Muire dhuit,* God and Mary be with you. *Erin go brách,* Ireland forever. Come Otherworld. *A phúca, tar i leith.* Carry this luggage-drift, wafting detritus in its hoodwinked bucket chug chug chug to market to casino, the world's fair wager wet-behind-the-lug-'oles, I'm spelled must never look back, never eat the apple, never open the box of pontoons on which I glide, unless, dear Reader, you kiss my gondolas, and whisper through our common walls.

FLYING SAUCERS

Same as every other day. Toy trucks looped back and forth on tiny tracks. Espresso machines puffed and hissed; operators banged grounds into bins. Toilets flushed. Cash registers opened and shut.

Passengers rifling magazines heard announcements. They talked on phones, stared into space. The flying-saucer man buzzed an upside-down bowl over their heads. With radio waves from his black box, he circled the saucer round his cart, landing it near rows of rubber helicopters, and robots that tumbled on faceless wheels. If Martians came to earth, he thought, they could shoot off in my saucers, and scoop ice cream or Mars Bars, they could play frisbee with people's hats.

He zoomed up the saucer again over the pop machines, over the head of someone in tight high-heeled boots and miniskirt, someone commanding her phone and marshaling her handbag and packages so they marched smartly along. Above her head he hovered his machine – a hat helicopter, a motorized halo. I wish, he thought, my halo would dissolve your boots and packages and fly us to an ocean beach, we would collect driftwood shaped like kingfishers, we would become driftwood ourselves, we would become the lovers of kingfishers, and the kingfishers would call over the waves till their lovers stepped out of the air as gods.

Just then the commanding person stepped out from under the halo and ordered coffee Americano.

SNOW

down steady down fall flake down by flake down round cloud-whirl tree by roof by frolicsome milk-wing flight-of-steps runaway runway quick lattice icicle faceted minikin clusters wittily mimical silica ventriloquy down by down by down doors porches by churches banks frosty postage to rustle and bluster downtown towers flour the tree-bark fringe the stones the hedges the wires the trellises tickle crystal thickety particle curriculum fill in footsteps fur the peaks dormers house-cakes blob fences banisters gates hat on a post hat on a trash bin a street lamp a cedar branch poof shushflump hat on a head blanket on a bedlam literal brittle obliterate sidewalk wheel-rut whited thickened bunting battened dada blanket saddle blanket muffled stumbled vacant hushed empty capricious neighbour-lot spatial suspicious vanished old-folk foundation feathery houseless mumbled duffled shushed to slant-wise slink millennial diagonal lamp-glow minutest snow-bees askewed crickle rupture flickety bugleg pitchy tick-tock letters flocking packeted jackets.

ON MY WAY TO THE OVERPASS

I see her in a sidewalk plaque, one of the Militant Mothers, stretching her arms across the oncoming train. Jean Amos, mother of five, of the Raymur housing projects. No more trains, she says in her warlike, combative way. No more will my children climb through couplings and wheels to get to school. No more kids vs profit – she speaks in her aggressive, overly political style of mothering, reminiscent of Joan of Arc. The railway men, well trained, yell at the mothers who have no right to be standing on their track: You'll go to jail, this is no misdemeanour, you'll be charged with a felony. Treacherous, cruel and fierce, the felonious mothers hold their ground, resolute as tracts of wasteland, firm in their perverse and wicked method of nurturing. The train, on its US Burlington Northern line, snakes passively backwards to the dock. Go to the City if you want an overpass, says the Canadian National Railway. I'll see you get criminal charges, mutters Inspector Beaten of Transport Canada to the biased, hard-line tenders of humanity. The arresting matriarchs are seized by police, who lock them up. Then let them go. The thing blows over with noble companies of railway men promising trains won't run from 8:30 to 9:00, noon to 1:00, 2:00 to 3:20. What distinguished

46

and high-minded companies – they even talk of an overpass. Not long afterwards, the trains snake back, stop beside the school. Children again climb through wonderfully shunting boxcars, hoppers and gondolas, resulting in a quarrelsome tent being pitched on the tracks by the bellicose, charity-receiving mothers. $1000 to stop your blockade, says a worthy company with goods for market. Jean Amos says, No. They've broken their promises, she tells the judge from which the venerable companies want an injunction. Let's make these promises part of my order then, says the judge. Thank you Jean, I say, to her bright mosaic chips, and I stroll over the overpass, over the trains snaking beneath my feet.

TANGLED RELATIONS

Dear Aunt, I'm sending you a drawing of a woman sitting under a tree and reading a book. In the book a woman is writing a letter to her aunt about the narrator. Dear Aunt, she writes, I'm in love with the narrator but the narrator is in love with the book. She's pining for it, waiting for the book to telephone in its fashionable way. I'm the woman in the book, I tell her, I'm the way the book comes to you. But the narrator continues to examine the telephone, unscrewing the ear-piece and mouth-piece and removing the switch-hooks, the finger-stop and the dial. It's got too much acoustic resistance, she says. What's that, I ask, looking up from the page of the book to some leafy branches overhead. It's the real component of deafness, says the narrator, the imaginary component is reactance. Are you sure that isn't real too – how're you going to fix it? Open the diaphragms, get rid of the permanent magnet. Will the book come through the telephone, will you read me and will I you? Dear Aunt, does love come in books, writes the woman in the book. Yes, yes, of course it does, murmurs the woman under the tree, gazing at the page. The narrator, too, stops and ponders this transmission. The telephone rings. For you, dear aunt, says the woman in the book,

An artist made a drawing of a woman reading this book under a tree. She wants to know whether you're the same aunt that she's writing to and whether we're sisters or cousins. Okay, hold the line.

HAVE A LOVELY TIME,

said the friends of the lawyer as they drove away from Lakehaven, Be sure to keep the house anchored to the ground and don't forget to take the budgie for a walk. What dear friends they are, he thought, leaving me their cottage for the weekend. He sat down at the table and began writing a memorandum of law defending the moon from the sun and the stars from the galaxy. *Oh how far you are my stars,* said the budgie. The lawyer looked out across the lake. Its vast flat surface shimmered to the mountains on the opposite shore as he considered fines for the sun's violation of the planets. *Plummeting plutocrats,* said the budgie, *Do you like Uranus?* I guess it's time for your walk, said the lawyer. He latched the budgie cage to a pole and carried it like a fishing rod over his shoulder. *Am I a tied fly or a dressed fly, a streaming wagtail or a spinning minnow?* Budgies can't talk, said the lawyer. *Get out of your thought-cage,* said the budgie. The lawyer did not speak budgie, although in a larger sense he was in conversation with one. He walked along the shore of the lake casting his gaze here and there, with its bobbers, sinkers and hooks. After a while he reeled in his line, returned to the cottage and hung the budgie cage on its stand. He leaned back in an armchair and looked out at the lake. It was now closer to the cottage. Its smooth surface had crossed the rocks of the shore and also the lawn. In fact the lake was lapping at the foundations, gently rocking the cottage like a boat. It lifted off and drifted away from land. I'll phone for help, he thought, but he was inside the budgie cage, chin resting on his knees, arms scrunched to his chest, and the cage was swinging back and forth on its hook. *Rockabye lawyer inside your egg.* The budgie zoomed into the walls tilting the cottage this way and that, *When the bough breaks, your cradle will zag.* The bird lounged in the armchair. *Then, my hatchling budgikin, you'll come out of your case.*

DIRECTORS CHANGE DIRECTIONS

Don't touch. Don't skateboard. Don't talk with your mouth full. Say please. Wear pink. Shave your armpits. Manage your anger. Walk on the right. Don't pick fights. Pick the ripe ones. Don't pick your nose. Pick up your clothes. Cross your t's. Cross your legs. Cross at the crosswalk. Cross your fingers. Don't cross the tracks. Don't cross your wires. Don't play with fire. Don't play hooky. Play fair. Buy a television. Wash your hands. Speak clearly. Don't bust the queue. Pay attention. Pay the piper. Don't run. Go to Mexico. Go to hell. Go for broke. Don't stoop. Wait your turn. Wear a brassiere. Don't be a smart-ass. Say excuse me. Don't turn into a pumpkin. Tell the truth. Brush your teeth. Don't wait by the phone. Look on the bright side. Smile. Don't get knocked up. Introduce yourself. Ask permission. Don't put up with it. Don't fall for it. Don't go to pieces. Get an A. Get a piece of the action. Get a life. Get your hooks into it. Don't get hooked. Hook up the television. Don't be late. Say thank you. Shop around. Don't pick the flowers. Jump off the deep end. Don't dig too deep. Jump on it. Lick the competition. Don't lick stamps. Don't get licked. Lick the sugar habit. Don't eat with your fingers. Jump on a plane. Hope for miracles. Cross off the list. Waste time. Dress for malfunction. Stay in bed. Backcomb the rubble. Eat the hand that feeds. Say fuck. Wear plaid purple. Get a Z. Undo the dress. Cook up a bandwagon. Sing with fights. Cross your televisions. Don't queue for pumpkins. Lie in the weeds. Lie with spunk. Give the lie to.

FABULOUS MODERNE

The city of All People had an apple tree in a piazza at the centre of town. A very old tree, at least 500 years old – some said 1000, spreading its stout branches over the grass and high in the sky. In spring, the people sang to the blossoms; in fall they danced apple feasts. Everyone filled their baskets. One day the tree was sawn off right at the ground – leaves, trunk, branches, all gone leaving only a vast round stump with hundreds of rings. Don't worry, the tree is still there, some said, You just can't see it. Don't be negative, they said, The spirit of the tree is still alive. There's plenty of food for everyone, and it's better than ever – now you can buy apple-flavoured bubblegum. Others said the tree had never been there; it was just a myth; it's always been a myth. Now that we have science and you can buy everything, they said, we have reality; you don't need myths. But we don't have money, people said, how will we buy food? Go to work at the sawmill or the logging camp or the coal mine or the shirt factory! But what will happen to our children and our elders; it takes a whole day to earn one piece of bubblegum. They can work too – just economize, the others said, this is the modern way. And the city was infested with a nine-headed Hydra, so poisonous its very breath was fatal. Hercules shot off the Hydra's heads with burning arrows. But for every head he shot, two more grew. It was his chariotman who sheared them off and seared their stumps.

SHE WOULD

fabricate what would come to be unreal and more real – a creamy morality that would automate. A concoction, a contraption. A buggy for stallions. It would have cosmic friction and helium arteries. The stallions would gossip over pyramids of gears, and the buggy would have wings. It would write itself in iron ink while the stallions, Bucephalus and Pegasus, recounted wars with chimeras and Indian kings.

How did you get those two-legged things on your back, Bucephalus asks. Minerva's golden bridle, Pegasus murmurs, I looked so good in it, excitingly winding around me its magnetic flux of elastic vibrations – until I threw off Bellerophon and kicked in the Helicon which they now call the horse fountain – ah, blushful Hippocrene with beaded bubbles. And you, dear ox-headed friend, with your great eye that conquered Persia, Anatolia, Syria and Phoenicia – Judea, Gaza, Egypt and Mesopotamia, how did they get on your back?

I was afraid of my shadow, Bucephalus neighingly laughs, but Alexander kept me away from its beaters and fly-wheels and flappers and pistons – I said to my shadow, Be gone! vamoose! and stormed the Persians at Granicus – and my shadow decamped – until I found its kingdom on the River Hydaspes – my shadow puffed up 10 times my size, its nose like a tree, ears like battle shields, and long white teeth clawing the cavalry – the stench of my shadow was foul, my shadow had multiplied – there were 50 shadows – I charged my shadows, biting and kicking like immortal Xanthus at the siege of Troy, but I fell with 4000 foot soldiers – and my shadow reigned.

She would. And she did.

DEAR MOM,

I've given birth to a tree and so at last you are a grandmother, and one day you'll be the great great great grandmother of a forest. How did I get pregnant with a tree, Mom. Was it from eating apple seeds? From climbing cedars? From drinking birch sap? Picking chestnuts, walnuts, hazelnuts. Carving my hearts in the oaks. I ate so many cherries and coconuts. From countless branches I hung by my knees. I think I'll never see a city lovely as my tree. Dear Mom, remember that windy-eyed man who gave you a silver snake. He's been knocking on my door. He offered me some inklings, smarts and know-hows. If he gave them to me, I had to promise to give something to him. I said No to his smarts. Then he offered me the latest most modern here-and-nows hot off the press, if only I would give this thing to him. No to your prestos, I said. I don't need your kitchen sink. Then how about a pack of trumpcards, a universal linchpin, all the keynotes and cruxes in the world and you the muscle queen, you the dominion diva. What do I want with your pullery, your cloutish aphrodisiac, I said, I have my little tree – Merrythought. Willy nilly bodacious. Willy nilly lexiludic. Biblio-baobab, my wishbone. Dear Mom, I pray no bonsai pots come near my tree. No nursery rows. No sidewalk holes. No rubber-tappers. No farming lumberjacks. Droogish oafs, oxters or boojums.

HIS SON, A CHILD OF THREE,

had died – eating zipnips – other children too – a GM virus bred with weed-killer. Zipnip Corporation did not withdraw the food from the market. The child lay in his bed wrapped in a shawl of ancient alphabets. I will take him back to Laconia, said Lycius the father, I will bury him in the old way in a meadow beside a mauve lake under an orange moon. The television factory, said his wife, You are foreman of R troop – the commanders will never let you leave. I will clone myself, said Lycius; they will never know. You must hurry – Zipnip officials are taking away the bodies – they say it's for scientific study. Open up, shouted a robot pounding the door, Health inspection! I will take him to Laconia, Lycius thought, as I did my father, though Zipnip Corp owns the lake, and the meadow is crawling with guards, my freeze-gun will make them statuettes. If they hit me with dope-gas, my neutron pellets will turn it to honeydew. I will take my son to Laconia and plant him like a seed; he will grow like my father into a twisty boa tree. His wiry arms will squeeze the Zipnip men to dust. Laconian soil will turn them to slime and feed them to androphages. Lycius was still thinking this when the Zipnip robots locked him down. His wife, the mother of the boy, ran from the house carrying the child in ancient alphabets. She crossed the five seas in a stolen laser jet and reached the Laconian border where Zipnip robots stunned her. As she lost consciousness she fired her freeze-gun. She awoke to furious statues and fled to the forest, found the meadow and the mauve lake under an orange moon and planted the child like a seed. So the boa forest grew 10-fold, as it did with every seed, and Laconia, which was part of a land once known as Canada, spread over the entire planet, many centuries ago, in the time of the Zipnip Wars.

GADZOOKS

Um. Hmm. Attaboy. Ah. Uh-oh. Oops. How odd. Lordy. What a corker. What a match. What an incredible show. Oh phooey. Oh pooh and tut. How ridiculous. Gee whiz. Hmm. Uh-huh. Mm-hmm. Mm-hmm. Uh-huh. What a coincidence that she met him there. How disturbing. Crikey. Gosh. What a thing. How common can you get. Oh really. Coo. Son of a gun, eh. Hmm. Mm-hmm. Uh-huh. What a relief. What a lucky break the gun was empty. Oh no. Oh my gawd. How appalling it took 12 hours. Bloody hell. Huh. Uh-huh. Hmm. Oh boy. How amazingly elastic the body is. Truly. Hmm. Now, now. Oh totally. Indeed. Totally. Oh my eye it is. My foot. What a trip. What a loser. What a complete lizard. Aw well. Oh dear. Oh hell's bells. Really. Hey, hot diggity dog. How marvelous she's leaving with the baby. Yippee. Well glory be. Bravo, bravo indeed. Whatever. Hmm. Mm-hmm. Mm-hmm. Ouch. Ow. Ow. Ow. What an idiot playing around with the saw like that. Oh really. Uh-oh. Shit. How awful they can't re-attach it. What a nightmare. Ah. Aha. Okay. Cool. Yum yum. Yummy. What fun. What a gas with the Smoothiacs and the Cyborginis. He he he. Whoopee. Ah. Oh no, yuck. Ick. How stinky. What a mess the barbecue'll be. Uh-huh. Uh-huh. Hmm.

Whatever. Oh rats. Shoot. Well, duh. How irrelevant to post an apology about the pink underwear. Oh bah. What a farce. What a pickle. What a bleep bleep bamboozler. How silly it went out as private and confidential. What a luscious kettle of fish. Good grief. Okey dokey. Ciao.

FROST

No beanstalk dude me. Nimble? Quick? Look for some other Casanova. Nor do I hang in pulpits or lanterns. I've never seen a playing card. And as for flat tires what would I want with those? Or asses or pines or cheese or rabbits. Squire of all trades – not me. I've only one. I paint, I imagine, I work and embellish – a spinster sent by stepmother into the forest – a lass, a wench, even a damsel I cover with silver acanthus, diamonds and crystals. Oh Femineity, are you warm, dear? Please, do have this furry muff, my girlishness – this fuzzy pom pom hat and blue-fox stole. And why not, my little womanhood, these thigh-high lace-up platforms. Come, my ivory gal, ride up on my charger – don't mind his icicles. Off we go to Castle Névé. Just one thing: never must you ever touch my staff. My wand, my baton, my walking shaft – please do not tap or brush, graze or nudge. Do not glance. Do not rub. Do not urge my impasto-painting rod. For if you do, my perfect cupcake, what will come? The most thoughtless impossibleness.

MAXIMAL

Don't cry over spilt milk. Don't cry over lunch. Don't cry on Wednesday, when cutting onions, or while shopping for a hat. Don't cry when you brush your teeth. Especially don't cry in an alphabet. Don't cry in banks or rivers, if you're on an island, or because of the post office. Don't cry in elevators when the buttons disappear in your hands. If you like carburetors, don't cry in a parts department. Don't cry into a gun. If you cry, don't drive. Whatever you do, eat your cake, because time's not money. And if you cry making love, cry in sentences. Don't cry in a maxim. Don't cry at you me, his hers, us them, human animal, nation dweller, profit labour, taker taken, ledger and song, past and future, fact and imagine a bath in a mirror, a plunge in a thought, a slip in a notion, a steep in a vision, a douse in an inkling, a soak in a picture because models speak louder than words, because all's not fair in echoes and alters, because clouds have silver hypotheses, because nothing supposed nothing inspired, and a rolling eye gathers its matter.

MY LIBRARY

Through this door you'll find my social science wing shelving aunts, uncles, grandmothers, grandfathers, cousins twice removed – my statistical bureau a.k.a. birth, ABCs, marriage, number of corn-flakes, toasters, irons, TVs, microwaves, hair curlers munched – my public relations' input-output, my wage-farm disability, childhood strikes and lockouts – pleasant peasantry, passenger freight in my wireless railroad, my secondhand cyclical warehouse of convenience psychology and shopping malls' chamber of coping skills. My odd-fellows' transvesticals, charity and life-saving accidents, once homeless, my teenaged blindness, my intemperate prison psychology, detectives, and correctional drug habits.

Now we turn to my technology branch including sanitary engineering, explosives and pyrotechnics. Feel free to browse the mobile food-processing servants running my living vehicle. Survey my soft furnishings, the mechanics of my weather instruments, while I construct tunnels and bio-acoustic floods. You can skim through my plasma. I have a fine collection of applied disasters. A first edition of my inland navigation. And

look at this waste reclamation plan with hydraulic dust-jacket –
soon I'll have fur, rubber, and leather volumes in my textile
zoo. And every edition of powerplant apparatus, its translations
to circuitry and plumbing. These decorative bindings bring
conditioners from all over the generator to fondle my sewing
machines.

This bay holds my will and choice including spirit messages,
clairvoyance and human / alien encounters. What fabric softener
have I not emoted with genius and class genetics. What cheerful
ridiculousness and vain fastidiousness, with my friends /
enemies, flattery and guilt, stitching up the most rational climate.
You'll learn how I control adulthood with applied hallucinations,
mesmerism and hauntings. How ancient, medieval, and modern
projections possess me with epistemological souls for space,
time and matter. Next to ethics, I've placed etiquette. Customs
and costumes. Party stunts and puzzles. Swords and parachutes,
maneuvering the phallic tropics with the latest neutralities. Not
that I wanted gabardine or burlap. Or this shantung leatherette.
For my seamless galaxy. No, far from it. It wasn't at all what I'd
imagined.

THE WIFE OF GASSY JACK

Madeline or Qua-hail-ya – his second wife. His first was her aunt. Gassy and aunt drive a Waggon Road, bed and table, yellow dog and whiskey, from New Westminster, paddle a dugout to Stamp's Mill. A board-and-batten saloon – the last one a Yankee traded for 4th-of-July firecrackers. At Luck-luck-ee maple trees, the sea's edge, mill-hands build a new Globe in a day. Gassy slings his whiskey and his bears, his scalpings, his shoot-outs. Granville town comes. The Commissioner of Lands puts the Globe in the middle of a street. Gassy and aunt buy a lot, build the Deighton Hotel, but aunt knows she's dying. You'll be his wife when I'm gone, Qua-hail-ya. Madeline's 12. A year later, she gives birth to a boy, he plays around Gastown, some say he's simple, they call him the Earl of Granville. The parlours, diningrooms and bedrooms of the Deighton prosper but not Qua-hail-ya's husband: his feet swell, his face turns muddy purple. They go back through the forest to New Westminster, back to his steamer *Onward,* up and down the river – leave the Deighton to brother Tom and Emma, *they* say Gassy doesn't have the gear to father that nick ninny. Is Gassy female? Or is he nothing but a coopered Siwash-lover. Emma throws a china teapot, calls him a beet-faced lush.

Madeline's husband sends Emma and Tom packing, but shortly afterwards, that plaque-renowned river-boat pilot, the father of Gastown dies, aged 44. Madeline's 17, the Earl 4. Lawyers tell her to leave, the Earl dies a few months later. The lawyers die, Tom and Emma die, Mrs. Qua-hail-ya Deighton lives on, raising a son, a granddaughter, weaving patterns in cedar baskets. An archivist comes, *to touch the person* of the wife of Gassy Jack, 82 in faded dress, rusty-stove cabin with cherry trees. Gassy Jack was your size, nice, good man, she tells him. Can I buy some of your cherries, he says.

MY CITY

Walking my streets L M N, 10 9 8, I've picked up prosaic slants and dramatic maxims. Set out habits racing to watermains. Connected pipes in my steam plant. Hooked up my sewers. I've found geography. My Latin quarter's *nomina locorum.* My barrio's *endroit.* My *arrondissement* of *Platzes, posti,* laid-down θέσεις. Not hazy ranges, not sweeps and wastes but *machtbereich's enceintes.*

Are περιφέρειά *Bezirks*? Are *lugares* sensible condominiums? What happens in these bailiwicks for sale? These lots and estates – do they speak table talk or play charades, my blindmen buff?

A thinker sits on a block. Oh how can I get off this block, he wonders. This stump, this jam. This likening of trolley buses to insects with antennae. These spelunking ruminations. Projecting paradoxes. Legislatures of colonies and suffrage.

And geography says, This is my yodel house. Would you like a window seat or an alphorn?

INVENTION 26

You plant a pole even taller than the Chrysler building right next to it. Then lasso the Chrysler, yank the rope tight, and run the long end over top of the pole. Hoist the Chrysler into the air. Swing it round, play tetherball.

Or melt a hole under the Chrysler, a de-elevator shaft. Slide the Chrysler into the ground – 77 floors, "Going down!" to the Lobby in China. Just the wedding cake of hubcaps sticking out above ground – a little art deco stainless-steel mountain. You could make the Cloud Club the Home of Stickiness & Clarity.

Or hinge it down sideways along 42nd Avenue past the Daily News and the Ford Foundation to the U.N. The world's largest hood-ornament, its longest javelin, narwhale, ice-pick. The largest traffic-calming nuisance and bother, cars running into it like ants to a steer carcass. People inside would step through the jaws of sidle-ators. "Going east! All aboard!" They'd colonize the horizontal walls and vertical floors of history on its side, crawling in and out its eye-sockets and fading ribcage. They'd settle in to its skeleton. They'd hang out shingles, clothes-lines and flags, set up cookstoves and potted plants. Grow a row of stalagmites from the gridwork of windows, a row of saplings from the fallen tree, a line of mile-high crenellated termite nests.

WIND

skitters leaves – tosses the hair of trees – it streams, scuds, hustles, jostles – tickling nips, mauling nuzzles – slap to flounce – wheel quiver twitch and writhe, scurry up, prod the clouds, the sea-pitch hullabaloo, tree-toss snap gung-ho bungle plunged at shores of rockrubble fecundity. Hunger. Monger. Tonnage bulldoze to hoodoo gloomy-gus foozle.

Mountains gully and gorge the wind limbs – crows, eagles wing-tip tracery, rush through brush of a spruce the mad craggy rake of cottonwoods – its gunrunning gallop plowed with skyscrapers, who groove it, channel it – sea-cool undulate nuzzle its topsy-turvy wall-smack, its bonks at steamy cumulonimbus buffoonery.

Rub a dub dub, wind to the house curries, scours, grazes, grinds – wind-grope fingers and thumbs fumble, stroke, twiddle, tweedle, cockeyed mono-moniasing saxophone omen – wind-fondle cobra locomotive. House plucks it, plays it, runs its finger to sweep of organ blithesome hushaby tentacle the house tongue, the house hook to flexing giving plumes elastic scuff and tug, fiddle and hold. House-catch a soupçon turbulent bump works its spur in sleek and billowy coilage. O rugged jolting house you burr, you plundering tooth to my amoroso, you strumming nipple.

MY RAT

I found a rat in my book bag. He wasn't very happy in his plastic wrapper – very anxious. I took him out while we waited to change for ballet. He was hungry. I showed him some tomatoes pocked like the moon. He rightly turned up his nose. I gave him a peeled orange, holding my hand flat so he wouldn't bite me. He loved the orange and was happier after that. Until we had to put on leotards and toe shoes. I am not a classical rat, he said. I'm not logical. I'm not smelly. And this is not about rats. If I were you, he said, I would avoid the subjunctive. Okay, I said.

SINGING LESSONS

You must go on the road and find singing lessons, my teacher advised. She was the chorus-master of a large opera, shaping and sculpting the elkish basses, the beaverish baritones, the tenor lynxes, the porpoiseful altos, the soprano loons. You have too many feet in your songs, she said, melt some on the road. Hike, amble, stride or stagger, anyway sing as you go. I went on the road. I took directions. Were they mine or the road's. We did not dispute the ownership. My puppet walked inside me, clacking mandibles, bonking knees and elbows. Go straight on, she said, veer off a little, make a sharp left and when you get to the castle look for the oldest woman. Hear the note in your head before you sing. Repeating a song caresses your brain. I met a rat practicing arpeggios, and humming, Music is the food of livers, Sing onion songs and bacon. Monday songs and Tuesday. A song in time makes nine, crooned a cow, Sing needles and thread, sing meadows and hey to the moon in a dish with a spool. Night fell. Walls fell and eggs fell. I met three bats flying over the road. We are eighth note, quarter note and half note. Each of us is half or two times one or the other, and together we are whole. Melody's on the road – where does it begin or end? To put echoes together again – all the song's horses and all the song's pens.

PUPPETS

Ah, what a puppeteer am I, my wires crossed, my puppets tangled. Oh do get up, stop acting like spoiled children. If you must be children I wish you'd at least be good children. Right ho, at your service, our wonderful puppeteer, here we all are nicely in a row, you can walk us and talk us, swing us and bounce us and hang us up. How we *love* bounces and hang-ups. And words put in our mouths. You daft puppets, you're perfectly wooden. We'd love to be natural for you, we can be spontaneous, artless, genuine and relaxed, we'll do anything you want. Get real, you can't *act* natural. Then we'll be bona fide and true, just say the word, your wish is our commotion. Ah you puppets are so goody-goody; I wish I had real puppets and not you silly clodhoppers. To go on or not to go on, that's what we'd all like to know, I mean should we put up with insults and snubs or take you down a peg. Take that and that you rat. Alas, poor puppeteer, I knew you well. Stop, stop, you dithering Danish prince, get your sword out of my ear; I'm not a rat behind the arras. Yes, actually there's a great deal of the rat in you. You chew, you make maps of your mazes; you make settings, characters, plots. Okay puppeteer, let's get this show on the road: up hand, up foot, up kneeser and header. Up elbow, up spine, up stomach and heart.

ALPHA

You stand – machine gun over your shoulder. Ammo magazine slung across your chest. Leather wrist guards. Leather trousers on your cocked hip. Leather bodice cupping your breasts. We were destined to meet under this red sky with your fighter jet beached near a sea of greeny milk while you pose for the lens constructing your lips. Your hair tumbles down your back. You wear arrows and mascara. How will you escape this picture? Your eyes glowing like blue lasers – if you look my way they'll stab straight through my ribs. Luckily you're not looking. You're glaring at your war, with an egg-sized ruby at your throat. Oh speak at least. Tell me what to do about your highlighter and the languorous lock escaping from your pilot-goggle tiara. What happened to us? Why must I, like a wind-tangled palm tree, burn for you? The nosecone of your jet, its glassy cockpit Operation Romance, penciling your brows, brushing your blush. You stand by your craft. I stand by mine. You smoulder, you stalk, you seethe. I refuse to be painted. You strike propositions. I recoil. The world's at your feet, it's on its knees.

A PLAQUE FOR FATHER

She's come 3000 miles to unveil it. Isobel Hamilton – 70 years old. A man screws a bulb into a camera. *I'm Isobel,* she thinks, *oath of Baal, god of flocks and fertility. Club-wielding grain-wielding god of sacrificed babies – him Phoenicians put on temples and tombs.*

Her father's plaque is fastened to the Bank of Commerce, a granite block of aluminum windows, across from the Dominion tower on Hastings Street. *Not me the child who was sacrificed – it was Mother, she was Isabelle too, not the god, but the offering.*

A man in a charcoal suit and fedora, *is it Thomson or Dodson,* tells her the mayor will lift the veil and shake her hand for the cameramen. Granite cobblestones of Hamilton Street glisten beside the Bank. Father's street. Lauchlan Alexander Hamilton. *Land of lochs, defender of men.* All across Canada, Hamilton Streets. All across Canada plaques like this one: To the First Land Commissioner, Canadian Pacific Railway 1885. Who "in the silent solitude of the primeval forest drove a stake into the earth and commenced to measure an empty land."

She sat on Mother's lap on fallen trees fat as elephants – trees towered around them sheltering them from the rain. Branches like giant wings, Mother said. Sheltering their wooden cottage with its wooden shingles. Mother's hands gathered her hair, combed it, braided it; Mother read her *Little Red Riding Hood*. See the word "red." The white curve of her fingernail touched three black marks. Isobel refused to walk in the forest. Refused to wear red. Mother gave her a lace collar that she'd had when she was little. They stood on seaweedy rocks. Look, Father's building a town.

Father's axmen chopped lines through the forest. Made roads of tree trunks. They burned the ground. Built hotels, trading posts, saloons and docks, churches and realty offices. The three of them paddled a canoe.

Dodson, or is it Thomson, holds an umbrella over her head, ushering her closer to the plaque. The mayor talks about the great city – By Sea and Land We Prosper – the great founder, Lauchlan Alexander Hamilton. *Why was I afraid of the tree-wing forest – Little Red Riding Hood had flowers in her woods. Her mother didn't paddle a canoe.* She's gone away, Father said. He sat on a log, staring across the water to his town. No she's never coming back. She can't come back. Isobel reaches to snatch away the veil. *Where's the plaque for Mother?*

Miss Hamilton, are you all right? *Yes, fine, fine – my ankle turned.* The veil's still down, her shout only in her head. His worship's shaking her hand. She's smiling at the camera, beside the brass trees on the plaque.

THE BAT EXPERIMENT

Bats aren't blind. They've got eyes. You're the one that's blind. I'm going to perform an experiment to help you see at night. Did you know that one quarter of all mammal species are bats? I'm going to put some bats under the bed-covers with you. Bats are not rodents. They're soft and furry. Their hands are wings that touch and hold. I want to find out how they'll fly in the cave of your sleep. What they'll do in your belfry. Will they ring your bells? And if they do, will you clatter, gurgle and snap, or hiss, boom, clink and whisper? Don't worry – if they bother you, call me on the bedside phone.

Are you sure bats would like to fly around in a cave? I think they'd rather hang upsidedown. I'll give them a coat-rack and hangers. I'll give them a picture frame, a rib cage, a clothesline, a storyline. And by the way isn't the job of the experimenter to see with her own eyes and hear with her own ears? What's this telephone?

Bats fly around at night discussing their hypotheses – the experiments we echo-locate in cries and mutterings. They ricochet and boomerang back. They make shapes in our brains, and we navigate the shapes. Without them we'd be completely blind.

ZIGZAGGY

You see how it's longer in front and shorter in back, I like that, I don't like his part in the middle, I like this one, it looks like Keira in the movie *Domino,* his is straight, mine's wavy, I like this feathery look on the side, I don't like nice, I like it rumpled, not too long, I like it breezy, like his, not woolly but squared, more fading out at the back, and combed over, tight sides and wavy on top, so it leans away, a little bit shaggy and hanging down, but sticking up at the top, in and out over the ears, zigzaggy and glossy, I don't like skinny, I like medium, not too shiny either, at the front I'd like it to curve, like Clint Ford's in *Exoskeleton,* but more rounded, not flat, I don't like cute and dangly, I don't like parts, I'd like solid, but toothed with not too many ends, a lop-sided shape with some notches, I don't like fringy, it should be high and firm, like Ethan Lynch in *Slime,* or Taloof in *Night Commando,* I like the layers in his and the tails, it looks raw instead of fuzzy, not his though, too smooth, too trim, too slanting and slick, at the back I'd like style, not thin or pointy, and sides not too low, more uneven, more bent, more crooked, his is like Thane McVeigh in *Haunted Mountain,* it's hard, it's jagged, and twisted off to the side, curvy like an arrow, I bet he's got girls, bet he doesn't even have to ask, they just flock around.

SLEEPLESS WITH VULGAR FRACTIONS

I'd like a permutation. It could be the most infinite set or it could be a vector. Maybe Monday's algorithm. Maybe the cardinal ones. Or I could try the irrationally functional. What should the skewness be? Should it be convex or concave? I'd like it to be four-dimensional. With polar coordinates but no multiples or factors. But that's too radical, too logarithmic. It's got to have cusps and nodes and rigor and parameters. Should I measure these on an interval scale? Or take the inverse tangent? I like Turch's topology, it's got smooth distortion, stretching and knotting. Did Turch tell Applebuns about Peeny's cosine? I must remember to prove Turch's premise before Peeny truncates. Before Boizo and Shurkoff plot their stochastic givens or curve their axioms the way Lazer did when we were filling the octagons with lozenges. I'd really like a permutation. It could be a collinear mirror or it could be a slope. Maybe Newt's recursion. Maybe a vulgar fraction. Or I could count the disjoint sets. How would I borrow an odd point? Could it be crude and random or wedged and solid? I'd like it to be polynomial. With ring-shaped shear but no similitude, no roots, class or brackets. But that's so finite, so non-negative. It's got to be slanted and elliptical and oblique and. Should I measure these in long divisions? Or find the assumed operators? I like Newt's vanishments, they've got maximum glide reflection. Did Newt cancel Lazer's postulate with Shurkoff's falsity? I must remember to cross-multiply Newt's paradox before Boizo transposes. Before Peeny and Applebuns square their hyperbolic tautologies or plane their signs the way Turch did when we were lining the real with truth. I'd like a.

DEAR POST-LAND,

I'm from Ontario but where am I addressed to? and where's Ontario from? Can it return there with address unknown? If Ontario goes back where it came from, where will I be? Can I still write to you from there?

Dear Post-land, In Paris, do I keep Ontario with London or with Iroquois or California? Should I put trilliums *on* it or *beside* it? Where do I put Ontario when I'm with Manitoulin Anishinabek? Or when I'm Hudson's Bay beaver flapping my James Bay tail?

Dear Post-land, Do you think Ontario looks like a hunchback staring into Lake Superior or more like an amoeba with vacuoles at Lake Nipigon and Lake of the Woods, with a pseudopod from Windsor to Ottawa? What's the pseudopod standing on? If it were a real foot, could it squash Niagara Falls?

Dear Post-land, If Canada were a computer, what address would Ontario have? Would it have to be right beside Manitoba or could it be anywhere on the hard-drive? The line through Lake Superior – would it be tied to the Canadian Shield or just other lines? Comic or tragic?

Dear Post-land, Do you think Ontario has a gender, and if so could it be a transvestite? When Ontario dresses up, who is he/ she loyal to? Are they loyal to heaven? Are you more loyal to Ontario or more loyal to Marilyn Monroe? Loyal to subjects or loyal to hailing?

Which post are you?

SUN

hides in a cave, a brother destroyed her rice fields, threw a skinned horse on her looms, a brother seduced her, a blind brother shot a bear and she got the head, he got dog meat, she goes under the world to the dead, sees with eyes of the dead, she cuts off her breast: sear it, eat it since you love my body so much, Sun grieves, faithless man-moon fucked her daughter, her morning star, dance dance for her amber tears, show her your breasts your vulva, build her a birth canal, a winter crack in megalithic hill, toothless Sun: strike my head into the well, Sun gouges her eyes: take them since you love them so much, o mirror mirror her wells, urns, brush her bloody sockets with rushes, your hair burns, you bulge huge, tabbycat, o rage rage red – princess in the sea, steal her, eat an egg but don't break the shell, leap to the fire, in the wolf's teeth, ladybug ladybug fly to your spinning troll luminous Saint Lucidity eating winter babies, give her pancake wheels, give her white doe's blood on birchwood braids, skin of the doe stretched hooped, sling-shot her house, steal her bag of thread, drive o drive your chariot over Olympus, μέδων Medea Medusa.

INVENTION 36

A boutique where you try on Mum's *Don't tell me* or Dad's *bamboozle*. Grandpa's *Howdy doody*, Grandma's *Good gracious*.

Try on skin. White. Black. Gold. Or sheer. A transparent handbag. Through which intestines coiling. Heart pulsing. Blood running.

Replace intestines with soil. Heart with molten magma. Blood with bacterial telephone lines.

Here, use the undressing room. My misfitifier will show you all the latest metasuits and matchistic snugitude for concrete walls, boardrooms and parties. Antivisibility's invisible. Its space-suit of silver windows hugs your shape.

Step into my mirrored room, turn around, turn inside out. Mirrors within mirrors disappear in this little transparency handbag. And while you're in there caper about, do anything you want: murder a tyrant, create a cure for human cruelty.

What outfit will you choose for birth and death, love and grief?
I'll measure your inside seams and crotches.

YOU COW,

a man said at a conference. You and your animal oozing, flooding. They swept him into another symposium. Symphony. To drink together. The woman-cow jumped, skittered. Hair long, black, flying out. *I am nervous,* she said. Black eyes, sad, aslant. Minerva ran her hands through the tangled hair. Journalists crowded round with notebooks. The woman-cow on four legs rustled tables of a cafeteria. Chairs. *These flimsy man-made things, I might shatter them,* she said, a judicious centaur who'd been stupidly shot with a poison arrow. The journalists brushed her tail and soothed her ankles. They gazed up to the stars on her belly. Stars where the centaur fled. *I am not a hooligan or a drunkard,* she said, *Be so kind as to bring me some blue radishes.* The journalists measured her towering legs. North. East. South. West. Daytime eating Big Bear Little Bear, the Bull and Bellatrix. Nighttime rebirthing them. Her cathedral chest and curtaining udders. The journalists marveled. Ladders, raise up ladders, they cried. Up to the stars. Let down your milk, let down your milk. *It is trapped in my father's turret.* Minerva caressed her. Oh let down your milk, she softly said. A galaxy poured down, and the journalists climbed to the sky of centaurs.

(ELEVATOR)

I step into its gilded, fluted columns. *Top floor, s'il vous plaît.* Wouldn't you rather go down, says the operator, there are many floors in the basement. All the pink floors are down there. *Up please, I'm renovating the apartments in the penthouse.* Floor three has very nice blue and pink arrangements. *I must work on my renos.* But you can't. *Why not?* This is the Patriarchal Hotel. Top floor's reserved for authority. I know it's stupid but I'm just the roast mutton riding up and down the dumb waiter. *I'll hire a helicopter and fly to the penthouse.* You can't, there's no outside to Hotel Patriarchy. *Look out the windows – birds – air – sky to fly through.* Yeah I know, but it's patriarchal birds, patriarchal air and patriarchal sky. *You don't have to be a mutton; you could choose to take me to the top floor.* Not with patriarchal choice. *How do you know this is the Patriarchal Hotel?* There's nowhere else to be. *Of course there is, Hotel Patriarchy* **is** *because of its* **isn't**. I'd rather live in the **is** than the **isn't**. *And it* **is** *because of its* **wasn't**. Yeah, but that's a patriarchal **wasn't**. *The hotel – how high is it – high as the moon, high as the stars? A patriarchal high? In patriarchal words, patriarchal wombs, patriarchal time, patriarchal silence, patriarchal thought, patriarchal matriarchs.*

I get off at the penultimate floor. Take the stairs up, and continue my renovations.

THE LAWN DRESS

scrubbed her words dirtily. She hung white li(v)es. White wall(et)s. White st(o)reets. White (grr)rooms. On the line. It's a good day for washingles, said a horse-dog over the fence. Yes a very fine d(el)ay. The Lawn Dress went on hang(ker)ing shee(p)ts and tow(e)els. Will you come with me to the car-navel, said the horse-dog. Nay, said she, I must soap my wor(l)ds before the man-iple comes home. Look at my pile of wor(l)ds; high as the heav(y)ens. I will hel(lu)p you – the horse-dog leapt over the f(eel)ence. No thank you – the Lawn Dress threw some p(r)ants and shir(le)ts into the sud(den)s. The horse-dog gallooped up the pile of wor(l)ds – she chewed them up, they were (trom)bones. My words are ruin(g)ed, go away god-dogged-horse, go away from my line(al)ins and cot-ton(e)s. Come to the craneval, said the horse-dog, I will glue your wor(l)ds. I will carol you on my back. I will take you on my marry-go-round. Just then the manner-man came in. These clothes, why are they torn up, he demanded. Why are they marked with letters? The Lawn Dress stood by her wash tub. Oh Manner Man, said she, behold my galleon. I am her pirate captain gathering golden-eyes and sil(ly)ver. We have come to Utropia for buried treasure, in a dark woo(le)d, 27 p(l)aces south and 36 p(al)aces east of the manner house in the c(r)ave of a drago(o)n. Stand back from my (s)words.

MY AGENCY

In my production studio, I throw back my shutters, meet my creative director. Copy writers swarm over us. I send them for new blood. My art department erects flyers for the latest campaign. Get image targets. Get juice and punch. Strategy. Tactics. My wanteds will be posters; my spots will be billboards. Let me poke digits into clients of myself.

Friction, force-fields, magnetism – I research. Dig up enzymes and yeasts. Get multiplication. Get logos. Map competitor apartments. Means. No. Trump. Yes. Authority. No. Coup d'état. Yes. Importance. No. Signify. Yes. Exert. No. Muscle. Yes. Rule. No. Sublimity. Yes. Clout. No. Conductive. Yes. Pressure. No. Dispatch. Yes. Use. No. Capacity. Yes. Force. No. Morph. Yes. Convert. No. Midwife. Yes.

False job-starts chides my traffic boss. I ring the phone of myself. Make weathercocks of myself. International Standard Self Numbers. Epaulettes and bugle calls. Ripen them, says my she. Brew them in my market niches, my slots and buttonholes. Your my is not my my, I say to my she. Your my is not her my just as my she is not her me, and my her my is not your my she. All the better to eat you with, my little she me, my sweet her your me in my wheel teeth.

Oh come to me my rifts and ha has, my honeycombs of surge and dint, for it is very dark in this stomach.

PARTS DEPARTMENT

I park the car and follow footprints underground. To a cave where lights flicker on blotches of grease. Mechanics in blue overalls. Air hammers, nut pullers, brake lathes and torque wrenches. A pry bar clangs the concrete. A man under a hoist under a car splays out his foot as he heaves his shoulder into car belly, grabbing pliers and clamps from his surgical tool cart.

I line up with a golfer, a lifeguard and a postal worker. Front-deskmen peer furiously into their screens at plate numbers. Print out work-orders in triplicate. Lube job. Brake shoes. Clutch overhaul. Timing. Super-easy slice cure, says the golfer's magazine. Sand game. Ball position. Control your trajectory. *If you see a line of flotsam moving seaward,* the lifeguard muses, *that's a sign of a rip current. They form around structures.* Should I sort shibboleths with passwords or with stamps, wonders the postal worker, Badges or tickets, blue ribbons or bunting? *Look for a break in the wave pattern or a channel of churning water.*

Among the blue bins and cardboard boxes of gaskets, pistons, and spark plugs in the canyons of the Parts Department, two grey-beards trade hugs, cheek to cheek, then the other cheek to cheek.

Your number is up, says a deskman, you'll have to stay here with us. *When you're caught in a rip,* warns the lifeguard, *Swim parallel to shore, then angle in to the beach.*

HEAT HAZE

Hills heads say. Hills hands hold. Hills hug. Hills hostage. They hang. Hundreds of hills hand dull. Huging. Dullarding. Hills holed up. Old eroded odours doldrums ponder horizon. Roads they row. Rows they Romeo, rows they rubáiyát, they rube, roads of ruins, of rules, rods of rudes, dunes jugged smudged muddle. They buzzard. The hills mongrel. Dull jugs of mudded clouds moan monu-mood. The dun hills hunge over haggard gullies. Gaze gooey. Greedy. Hill heavy. Heave vee. They hang-dog hum mid. The hills gradual glue. Megalo bung. They midden mod-bulls mod duels. Megalo blued booms. They haggle. Hand bond to head. Bed to mumber. Mono gaga to molybdenum.

Old eroded hills arrange. Arraign, they say, array. We want arraigning. Play our faces. Lathe our longwave lupine faint faded faze. These our ranges, our mundane labours braided daze unable us, unlake us, unladel us in caged muscle. Assail us in layers lately sliced flanges. File our irons. Untied we wait, we old eroded tired whales. We make brigades line up our lions, our lagging luggard lions to file. Five of them stoop and rake ruins flake and fail. Stoop pad, stoop pud. River ground. Tired whale fire. We muggle ground-weary baleful sluggishness corroded old draggy gauges.

Us drones the recondite information highway. Us woolgathers rabbit / gopher this whirring transportation monotony ribbon. Interpretational thistle ideation trucks us pensivelessness. Essential expresswayed. Us transcendental vague quintessential coyote.

HOTEL

A red building. I in my black cape. I remember in the bar an artist sketching an actor rehearsing her lines: Oh messenger, speak! [*gazing into mirror behind bottles of Crème de Menthe and Kahlua*]

Messenger:	Here's the unmessage.
Actor:	Who sent it, how did it get here?
Messenger:	Orphan lines on my sketch-pad.
Actor:	I hear you; there must be a message
Messenger:	a darkroom development
Actor:	a story
Messenger:	a reflection
Actor:	a sketch
Messenger:	in the mirror of a bar
Actor:	in a hotel
Messenger:	in the dreams of quixotic memory
Actor:	there's a mistake in the lines.
Messenger:	You've crossed the wires.
Actor:	The hotel is wired.
Messenger:	The hotel's full of echoes.

Actor:	You're supposed to act as though it isn't.
Messenger:	You're supposed to pretend to be acting.
Actor:	How do I get out of it? How do I leak from phantom corridors, palmy salons, room service, bellhops, maids. Check in, check in, check in. To Moscow. To Paris. To Hong Kong. To Mumbai. In five-star language. Always for a few nights that stretch to other nights, nights overlooking the sea, the train station, the piazza, the market. Nights with keys and windows. Nights with baths or showers or buckets. How do I return to my sketch-pad, a black caper, a red edifice, and the time beyond dreams?

SEWING

In Home Ec the teacher Mrs. Shears spreads Simplicity patterns over our fabrics. I was always going to be a fashion designer, she says, or a linguist, or an astronomer. I was going to be the one who would create these quick and easy blueprints. The one to be a star. I could be a whole constellation. Be careful to pin your fronts with the grain of your cloth, Mrs. Shears continues, Did you know that Andromeda is a chained woman? For her mother's boasting. She whose name means *think of a man* – her father bound her naked to the beach to appease a sea-monster. Life is simpler in our modern age. Cut your notches in surrounding material, not your shirt. Did you know that in her autobiography Andromeda writes, *It wasn't some wing-sandaled man dangling a head of snake-hair who saved me from the sea; it was a Minoan Queen. **She** taught me to box and wrestle and leap the bull. Together we branded the labrys at besotted Athenian Zeusnics. Our phalanx of women shot them with arrows, keeping home safe for our men. And by the way that stuff about Amazon archers cutting off their breasts is a lot of old man's tales. Amazon – a mazing zone, we bring the mind to its senses.* And so we piece reality together, continues Mrs. Shears. Match your sleeves to your shoulders. Baste your backs to your yokes. I've always loved the word *pliers*, says Mrs. Shears as we stitch our collars and pleats.

BLACKIE PINKHEART

Armsco was neither owned nor rented, owned nor operated, owned nor funded, owned nor controlled. It was neither world-shaking nor trivial, neither intelligent nor amusing. That humanity exists it neither asserted nor precluded. That its products were dangerous to humanity, not to mention life in general, it neither verified nor guaranteed. It neither endorsed nor supported the planet. It said that neither Armsco nor its employees were responsible for the weather that persisted in falling. Rain and sleet neither reveal nor conceal anything, it said. We neither accept nor solicit snow and drought.

Blackie Pinkheart dwelt in a land that was neither city nor countryside. This in-between with its culture neither superorganic nor the handmaiden of genes – that Armsco made component X and component Y with men who were neither free nor slave – Blackie mulled over and mused on. He himself was neither a doormat nor a prostitute, pedantic nor wild, consenting nor protesting. He was neither certain of busybodies nor firm about nobodies. Neither welcome nor waif, Tweedledum nor Tweedledee. In his study of basal ganglia in mice, Blackie found neither pretangles nor post-tangles. Yet he thought a great deal about angles and was deeply moved by the fact that dark matter neither emitted nor reflected light. This is what spurred him to infiltrate the neurofibres of Armsco with neither evaders nor apologists or other third parties, filehandles or simple scalar variables. No longer would Blackie Pinkheart be told by presidents that Epicureans and Stoics were neither citizens nor patriots.

MY CHARACTERS

My sidekick muscles my henchman, whose hunter suspects my penitent who rescues my liar and his nephew, the prime minister, yet woos my cousin's worshipper and betrays his road buddy, her ex-dentist and the worshipper's daughter who cheated their boss in the hockey pool. Then the sequel: my stand-in star, piloting my princess's aunt to victory over his professor and their doctor who plan to jail my queen sorcerer with her slaves' bogus master conspirator whose sister abandoned my twin sons' karate teacher in my torturer's dumpster. *I don't find it the least bit crowded in here.* My karate teacher snaps a roundhouse, making her narrator duck under her mother's suitor and prudent villain who polluted our fake sage and his narrator's playmate with a billionaire. Your character pinched my dog, barked his narrator. To his majesty's apologist. In the pigpen. *Your* narrator ditched my Olympic diver for the roulette spinner. Oh my narrator, my narrator, I've lost her, breathed my acrobat. Where's my co-pilot in the legislature, my ex-neo-stunt-woman voice-over? *I don't find it the least bit crowded in here.* My karate teacher whips a side heel-kick my post-ersatz quack narrator fails to duck.

GREY

Always the white noise of my boss, the chalk walls and alabaster windows, the ledgers the colour of teeth, stack the sheets, keep the sheets stacked, now roll them out to shipping, get another batch, keep the sheep walking up the ramp, pull off the petals, the lily petals, the rabbit petals, the pearly petals, the ricey petals, throw away the stalks, don't talk, just do, do, do. Do it platinum. No ink, no! never do I want to see ink. Never do I want to see coal. Never do I want to see raven. Never ebony. Never jet. Never soot. Never tar. Look at my snow. Look at my milk. Look at my swan. My narcissus. My eyeball. Boss, I am crow. Shut up and do. Boss, I am shadow, I am slate. Shut up, box the ivories, mark the ledgers. Boss I am midnight, I am pitch, see me Boss, I am charred silhouette. Shut up, Subaltern, and count the eggs into their cotton puffs, and when you've done that, pack up my ledgers, clean out my desk, and say goodbye to me, because you will now be boss, and you must fire Grey. I boss? I in the head desk? I run the ledgers? free from the white noise and alabaster windows?

I went to Grey's desk. Grey the gun-metal thundercloud, Grey who faithfully stacked, counted, rolled out, shipped and reported, Grey the mousey, ashen, donkey-smoke who morning noon and night kept sheep and rabbits walking in milky tapioca. Grey, I said, I am sorry. I reached out a hand. We held hands across the desk and looked into each other's eyes for perhaps the only time. A terrible plow had cultivated the cheeks and forehead of Grey. Will you be alright, I asked. We still held hands. Still looked into each other's faces. Furrows. I'm sorry too, Grey said, at the end of the day I do like you, I never thought I would, but I do, I like you very much. Goodbye, I said.

THE SONIC BOOM CATCHER

I've always wanted to cross the sound barrier, Kaspar said to her friend Sigismund. It's greener on the other side. It's friendlier. Not that it's not friendly here with you, it is, but I'm certain it's more furthering on the other side of the barrier, more tending and availing to inventors and ingeniuses such as we. No, not a word (she held up her hand), you're going to say I can't possibly know since I've never been there. You're going to tell me stories of Icarus. But remember, Daedelus also flew away from his island jail, and landed safely in Sicily. I've delved into this, I've looked at it and fathomed. If I catch a sonic boom, I'll cross the barrier. I know where one hangs out. I tracked its spoor of scorched ideoglyphs. Its signal stench. I found its circles in the field where we tested dreameanors.

Kaspar raised her nets of muzzlements and dumbitures. They covered the whole sky and sure enough when the sonic boom came the nets caught it. A thousand hurricanes thrashed inside the snare, tsunamis boiled the ether filling the world with a terrible silence. A tonguelessness. Lightning without thunder. Earthquake without rumble. Not a bray. Not a twitter. Not a hiss. Not a nicker. Only a tomb of violent quietude. She must open the nets, she must let go the sonic boom, but the nets were so glutinous, so barbed, so leechy, so lovably kickbacked. She must wait more patiently, she thought, she must not really want that notness that she was not forbidding, the not of what she unwanted that she was uncarelessly not insouciant to, the not of what she didn't know but which she was compelled to unseekingly diswoo.

FUTURE PAST

The past is coming. It's going to have arrived. The past will be a bed with no stead, its legs evaporous, its mattress imponderable. Perfect, imperfect, more than perfect, it will be tense. It will be going to have been tense. You'll sleep in this edgy. You'll make love in it. On its sheets, you'll find spots. You'll read books in it. Into it you'll be born and give birth. You'll make it and rumple it. You'll die in it.

The past is coming. It's going to have been eating and talking, talking and eating. It will be retroly progressical. Precooked, postcooked, anticooked, the past will be your trophy. It will be succulently necessary. You'll waffle in it. You'll portion it out, even ration it. Milking its magpies, you'll soliloquize, and sandwich its muttering balbucinations in saucy falafels. It will butter you up; it will pickle you.

The past is on its way; it's going to have been coming. It will field, as in question. The past will crest and trough. Through its turbines, it will conduct inquiries and scoping zones. You'll rise and fall on its erections. In its sediments you'll corkscrew hither and thither. You'll dawdle, flit, halt, then dash, eke, linger, and saunter. The past will spread you out in thistles and clover, tides of neverness, everness, now a tussock, now a turf, now a clump, now a windrow, now a mouse, now a mole, now a snake, now a toad. Now the future is past.

NOTES

THE PLACKENER: *Placken* (Mid. Dutch): to stick or paste together, to piece together, leading to English *placard, plaque.* *Martingale:* straps attached to a horse's girth and bridle.

MY NATURE: adscititious = added from without, supplemental, not essential.

HE IMAGINED A SEAWALL: suidhe = seat in Gaelic.

ISLANDS: *phúca:* vocative form of *púca,* vampires, she-devils; *tar i leith:* come here; lug 'oles: (U.K.) lug holes, ears. The harbour ferries in Vancouver have suggestively Irish names. Originally I included other Irish phrases such as *taibhse,* ghosts, *spiorad,* spirits, and I translated *púca* as pucks, hobgoblins. However, my guide in all things Irish, Maurice Scully, advised me that although *púca* and *taibhse* are "haunting spirits from the otherworld as we understand them in English," *púca* is "almost wholly negative (& scary)" while *spiorad* "is mostly religious." He told me that although "dictionaries will tell you *pucks & hobgoblins* for *púca,* ... . hobgoblins belong to kiddie cuckoo land in our language-world whereas in Irish, it's something different. Culturally speaking, rather than linguistically, maybe vampires & she-devils might be closer as having some 'reality' in anglophone culture."

FLYING SAUCERS: In the halcyon days of winter solstice the seas are calm and according to myth the kingfisher (halcyon) nests on the water. Alcyone threw herself into the sea when her husband Cyex drowned. She was transformed to a bird and carried to her husband by Aeolus, the wind. "The Gods their shapes to winter-birds translate," writes Ovid.

SHE WOULD: Bucephalus was Alexander the Great's horse. Pegasus was ridden by Bellerophon to slay the chimera. At the Battle of Hydaspes River, Alexander fought Raja Porus, king of Paurava in the Punjab of ancient India. Porus used war elephants. Xanthus was Achilles' horse.

MY CITY: *nomina locorum:* Lat. place names; *endroit:* Fr. place; *posti:* Ital. places; *machtbereich:* Germ. sphere of influence; *enceintes:* Fr. enclosures; περιφέρειά: Gk. peripheries, region; *Bezirk:* Germ. district; *lugares:* Port. places; θέση, θέσεις: Gk. place, places, cf. thesis.

INVENTION 26: The spire on top of the Chrysler building is 122 feet long. The top floor once held the Cloud Club.

DEAR POST-LAND: The word Ontario derives from a First Nations word meaning beautiful water. In 1641 it was first applied to land nearest the easternmost great lake. It was applied to the whole province in 1867. Ontario's motto: loyal it began, loyal it remains.

SUN: Medusa's name comes from μέδων (medon) meaning ruler. Ancient people worshiping a sun goddess some 3000 years BC built a tumulus at a place now known as Newgrange, Ireland, capturing sunlight precisely at the winter solstice. Female deities representing the sun are found in Japanese, Scandinavian, Inuit, Baltic and other mythologies.

YOU COW: Bellatrix: very bright star in Orion, radiates 6400 times the light of our sun. Rapunzel means "blue radishes". Nut, the Egyptian goddess, sometimes takes the form of a cow.

SEWING: Labrys: a double-edged axe carried by Minoan warrior-priestesses. Perseus supposedly rescued Andromeda after slaying the Gorgon. Notches on printed patterns enable the stitcher to match up the pieces of a shirt at the correct points.

THE SONIC BOOM CATCHER: Jack Spicer in "Dictation and 'A Textbook of Poetry'" says "You have to not really want not what you don't want to say."

ACKNOWLEDGEMENTS

I would like to thank the editors of the following magazines in which pieces from this book have appeared or will appear: *Golden Handcuffs Review*; *Windsor Review*; *West Coast Line*; *Dandelion*; *Matrix*; *Event*; and *The Capilano Review*. Thanks as well to Mona Fertig and Harold Renisch for including "Future Past" in the anthology *Rocksalt*.

Warmest thanks to Jenny Sampirisi, whose patient nudges led to many fruitful changes in the final manuscript, and also to Jay MillAr for his dedication to Canadian letters and stunning book design. Thanks to Fred Wah, for encouraging me to take this project to Sage Hill, and to Sage Hill Writing Experience for giving me the opportunity to work on the book with Nicole Brossard. My warmest thanks to Nicole for all her suggestions and encouragement, and her inspiring talks about writing. Also abundant thanks to Karen Houle, Sandy Ridley and Tracy Hamon for their responses and suggestions in the baking heat of the Saskatchewan summer. I am also very much indebted to my Dublin friend Maurice Scully for help with the Irish phrases in "Islands." And thanks so much Colin Browne for your suggestions on the reference to Sḵwx̱wú7mesh in "He imagined a seawall."

I'm very grateful to Paul Auster and Siri Hustvedt who generously permitted Susan Bee's painting *The Red Door* to appear on the cover. I was thrilled and honored when Susan Bee agreed to make some drawings to accompany these texts. Thank you Susan for your support and enthusiasm and the delightful pieces that emerged.

Last but greatest thanks to Peter Quartermain, for whom mere words will never say enough.

MEREDITH QUARTERMAIN

was born in Toronto but grew up elsewhere in Ontario and in rural British Columbia. At UBC she was intrigued by the poetry of Jack Spicer and Robert Duncan. She also delved into Biology, Latin, Math, Philosophy and Linguistics. For a while she practiced law. She is the author of several books of poetry including *Matter, Nightmarker* (finalist for the Vancouver Book Award) and *Vancouver Walking* (winner of a BC Book Award). She runs Nomados Literary Publishers with husband Peter Quartermain.

COLOPHON

Manufactured in an edition of 500 copies in the fall of 2010. Distributed in Canada by the Literary Press Group: www.lpg.ca. Distributed in the United States by Small Press Distribution: www.spdbooks.org. Shop on-line at www.bookthug.ca

BOOK
PRODUCTION
WAR ECONOMY
STANDARD

Type + design by Jay MillAr
The Department of Narrative Studies is edited for the press by Jenny Sampirisi.